THIS UNICORN BOOK B

....

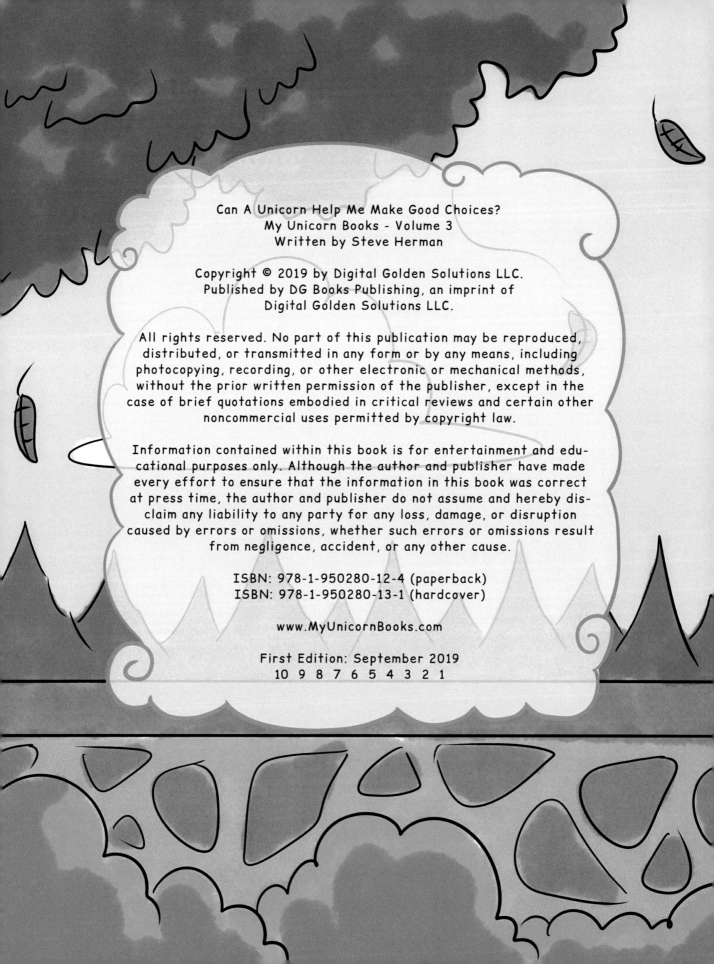

Can A Unicorn Help Me Make Good Choices?
My Unicorn Books - Volume 3
Written by Steve Herman

ISBN: 978-1-950280-12-4 (paperback)
ISBN: 978-1-950280-13-1 (hardcover)

www.MyUnicornBooks.com

First Edition: September 2019
10 9 8 7 6 5 4 3 2 1

Hi, my name is Allie, and this is Dazzle D.
The D stands for "Delight," and she's a friend to me.
You can see she is a unicorn, magical and rare;
We dance upon the rainbows and the clouds up in the air.

The time I spend with Dazzle D is like a holiday,
But there's another reason that I'm glad she came to stay —
When I misbehave, or I'm not acting very nice,
Or when I feel unhappy, Dazzle gives me good advice.

Would you like to hear a lesson that I learned from Dazzle D?
You might also need to learn it, too! Let's see if you agree!
We were at the city park a week or two ago,
Playing like we always do, but I was naughty, though!

I ate a piece of candy, then I took a look around,
When I saw no trash can, I threw the wrapper on the ground!

Dazzle D said, "Allie, what an awful thing to do!
Imagine what if everybody littered just like you!"

"Ben cried and told mom, so she put me in time out,
Although anyone can see it was all Ben's fault, no doubt!"

"Ben always takes my toys, but he never asks me first;
He loses or he breaks them, and that is even worse."

"And if that wasn't bad enough, later that same night
Another bad thing happened that I thought wasn't right."

"Dad was supposed to read me a book before I went to bed,
But he was on his laptop, working late instead."

"But my dad frowned at me and marched me down the hall,
And sent me off to bed with no bedtime book at all!"

"But then when Patty Peters dropped her pencil on the floor,
I stepped on it and broke it, and I found myself once more
Making someone angry; though I didn't mean to do it,
Since I didn't say, "I'm sorry," folks told me that I blew it!"

"I always have a reason for the choices that I make,
But no matter what I do, it seems I've made a big mistake".

"Now everyone is mad at me – Dazzle even YOU!"
Then I began to cry and said, "What's a girl to do?!"

"I understand," said Dazzle D, "why you are upset,
But here's some good advice that you should not forget –
Although you feel it's not your fault, perhaps you should admit
That there are better choices that you can make
to help out just a bit."

"Then Ben will give it back to you whenever you are done, And instead of being punished, you'll find you're having *fun!*"

"And when you closed your dad's laptop, what did you expect? Of course, you got in trouble, for you didn't show *respect*."

"Our parents must work very hard, and sometimes even late; Allie, be more understanding and be patient as you *wait*."

"When you broke Patty's pencil, though you didn't mean to do it,
It's not hard to say, I'm sorry – There's really nothing to it.
Just treat other people how you want them to treat you.
Imagine that you're in their place – It's the proper thing to do."

"When you are at the park and need to throw your trash away
Don't drop it on the ground; there's a much better way."

"If you can't find a trash can, take the wrapper home with you. Think of how the world would look if others littered, too?!"

"Allie, pay attention, and don't make the mistake
Of not being careful of the choices that you make."

"Don't go blaming someone else for what you've done,
For choices come with consequences – every single one."

So I decided I'd try out what Dazzle recommended –
I was pleasantly surprised to find out just how splendid...
Things turn out when you take the time to think
before you act;
Life has been much easier, and that's an actual fact!

And that is how I learned that I always should *think twice*
To make good choices and choose to do what's nice.

Dazzle D gives good advice, and I cannot deny it.
If you don't think before you act, I suggest you try it!

Get your FREE Gift from Dazzle at
www.MyUnicornBooks.com/gift

READ MORE ABOUT
ALLIE AND DAZZLE!

VISIT WWW.MYUNICORNBOOKS.COM

Made in the USA
Monee, IL
05 August 2023

40472926R00029